W9-CAW-227

To my sister, Martha,
a brilliant star by any measure.

Book design by Sara Gillingham.
Typeset in Nicolas Cochin.
The illustrations in this book were rendered in watercolor.
Printed in Hong Kong.

Library of Congress Cataloging-in-Publication Data available.
ISBN 0-8118-2854-9

Distributed in Canada by Raincoast Books
9050 Shaughnessy Street, Vancouver, British Columbia V6P 6E5

10 9 8 7 6 5 4 3 2 1

Chronicle Books LLC
85 Second Street, San Francisco, California 94105

www.chroniclebooks.com/Kids

Twinkle, Twinkle, Little Star

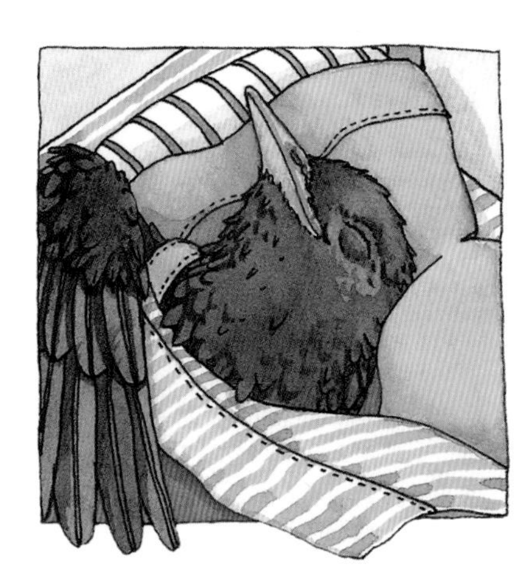

A Traditional Lullaby Illustrated by Sylvia Long

chronicle books · san francisco

Twinkle, twinkle, little star,
How I wonder what you are.

Up above the world so high,
Like a diamond in the sky.

When the blazing sun is gone,
When he nothing shines upon,

Then you show
your little light,

Twinkle, twinkle,
all the night.

Then the traveler in the dark
Thanks you for your tiny spark.

He could not see which way to go,

If you did not twinkle so.

In the dark blue sky you keep,

And often through my curtains peep,

For you never shut your eye,

Till the sun is in the sky.

As your bright and tiny spark
Lights the traveler in the dark,

Though I know not what you are,

Twinkle, twinkle, little star.

Taylor, Jane.

Twinkle, twinkle, little star.

$13.95

DATE